Running Mates

Withdrawn

Running Mates

by Libby James

Libby

1

Libby James

Penstemon Publications
Wellington, Colorado

*For Henry who reinvented himself.
And to Jane Welzel and Doug Mason
for inspiration everlasting.*

Thanks!

To steadfast friends in the writing and
running communities with gratitude for
their support and encouragement.

Libby James

Other titles by Libby James:

Muffin Magic, a picture book for four to eight-year-olds

Coming soon:

Frisbee Dreams by Libby James

Lauren Luster, a nail-biting, underachieving, overweight couch-potato, surprises her four "jock" siblings when she evolves into a sleek, self-confident sixth-grader. Her skill with a Frisbee, her dog, and her relationship with a retired football coach who becomes her mentor, all play a role in her transformation.

4

Reader comments

"Henry is the kind of kid I love to watch as a coach. In this brief story, James creates two lovable characters who grow and learn together by putting one foot in front of the other."

T.S. Berger, two-time Rocky Mountain Regional Champion, Olympic Trials qualifier, coach for 40 years. "Rip City" and "Start slow and taper off" are favorite sayings.

"Running Mates is an inspiring, charming story about running and the relationship between 13-year-old Henry and his adventurous grand-mother, Gert. Together they train for a marathon, a journey that trans-forms both of them."

Cathy Utzschneider, silver medalist, Nike World Masters Games, seven-time USATF national age-group champion, Author of *Mastering Running*, 2014.

"Running Mates is a story full of sweetness, tempered with the raw, unfettered truth of what it takes to be a distance runner. It reminds the seasoned veteran and beginner runner alike of the triumph of the hu-man spirit over the "nagging insecurities" we all confront as kids, or as fifty-plus year-old athletes starting a new sport. It is at once a "com-ing of age" story for a granny and a middle school boy, both of whom find that in their vulnerability, lies their strength. As you read it, you will smile in appreciation of James' ability to give voice to the sacred and transformational inner journey which perhaps we runners too often take for granted: that of metamorphosis from 'thinker' to 'do-er.'"

Melody Fairchild, first U.S. high school girl to break 10 minutes for two miles. Olympic trials qualifier, women's winner, Colorado Half Marathon, 2011, masters winner, Freihofer's Race for Women, 2014, Leadville, CO, 10k women's winner, record-breaker by four minutes, 2014. Holds the USATF masters records for the 5k, 10k, 15k and half-marathon, 2014.

The students at Elsmere Elementary School in New York state read Running Mates and principal Kate Kloss shared their comments:

"This story seems great for kids in grade 3 or older. Younger kids might not realize how much perserverance was needed in this story."

"The running tips you put in your story were great ideas for anyone who likes to run in races."

"The scene where Gert falls might be a little scary for some kids, but I liked it. Did that happen to you?"

"I run on the cross country team and, at first, running was really hard. Although Henry was just starting, it did not sound like it was so hard for him. Is it easy for some kids?"

"I was glad that Henry started to be proud of Gert. It kind of made me mad when he was embarrassed about her."

"Where are Henry's parents? Do they come to his meets? The only time we see his mom is when Gert gets hurt."

"Do Gert and Henry end up running the Boston Marathon?"

"This story made me want to join the cross country team."

Chapter 1

“What's all the racket, Henry?” Gert asked as she grabbed my arm and headed toward her front door. She wore raggedy black pants and a white T-shirt, and her wiry gray hair flew all wild around her face.

My friends all called me Hank, but I was always Henry to my “in-your-face” granny. “Dunno, Gert. Thunder maybe?” I yawned. “Or a herd of elephants?”

I'd just a minute ago rolled my thirteen-year-old body out of bed, and I wasn't exactly sure where I was on this warm August morning. Then I remembered: I had spent the night in my Grandma Gert's little brick house with the purple fence around it.

Just as the sun sent a beam of pale yellow light through the picture window in the living room, we'd been awakened by a steady pounding noise coming from the street. It went on and on until we both got out of bed to see what was happening.

When we opened the front door and stepped onto the porch, we saw people—all kinds of them—old and young, fat and thin—tall and short passing by in a great big herd. One of them waved and

7

called hello! A tall skinny guy clutched a cowbell that clanged as he moved. A short, round man held a cell phone high above his head blasting loud jazzy music.

"Stop!" I called out. "What in the world are all of you doing?"

"Running a marathon," a woman in very short shorts and fluorescent socks that came up to her knees answered, flashing us a grin as she went by.

"How far are you going?" Gert wanted to know.

"Twenty-six-and two-tenths miles. It's going to take us a while," the lady replied with a friendly wave before she disappeared into the crowd.

"Twenty-what did she say, Gert?" I wasn't sure I'd heard right. I would never in the world do that, I thought to myself. I had more than enough trouble getting through three miles of cross-country practice every afternoon for my middle school team.

"Seems impossible, doesn't it, Henry?" Gert frowned and slid a boney hand through her wispy hair. "How in the world do people do that? And there are so many of them."

Early the next morning, I was snuggled down deep in my own cozy bed when Gert and Tucker, her skinny mutt of a dog, stomped into my room without knocking. Gert lived only a few blocks away from me. Sometimes it seemed a little too close, and this was one of those times. "Wake up," she demanded in that loud voice of hers.

I pulled the quilt over my head. "Gert, don't you know it's Sunday?" I mumbled. "Leave me alone."

Then she bent down, close to my ear, tugged away my quilt, and went on just as loudly, "Henry, I need to learn about marathons right now. What do you know about them?"

I learned a long time ago that there was no stopping my round-faced granny when she set her mind to something. My eyes were still closed but I knew that those fierce blue eyes of hers were piercing right through me as I lay there and I knew there would be no more sleeping for me.

"I don't know much of anything about marathons, but we both know they're long, right Gert?" I turned my back to her, but she wasn't about to give up on getting me out of bed.

"Get up," she commanded. "Tucker and I need you to jog around the lake with us."

I loved my Granny Gert, but sometimes I wasn't sure how much I *liked* her. When we went out to eat, she embarrassed me when she asked for extra stuff like more rolls and extra cheese and pickles. And she always asked in such a loud voice. If her food wasn't just right, she sent it back to the kitchen.

But the trips we took together were the best. Once she took me to Alaska to fish for salmon. Another time she took me to Disney World.

"Too early," I groaned, as I dragged my tired body out of bed. Running had never been my idea of fun. I only did it because I had no choice. I especially wasn't up for a run on a sleep-in day. But I knew my granny. She wasn't going to let me lie in bed for another second and there was no way in the world to change her mind.

"Okay, let me see if I can find some shorts." I dug into the mountain of half-dirty clothes by my bed and pulled out a pair of almost-clean cut-off sweat pants. I splashed cold water on my face, and without even a zit-check in the mirror, I followed Gert down the stairs, pulling on my favorite yellow T-shirt as I went. I grabbed a baseball cap to clamp down my sandy-brown curls, and hopefully hide my face a little.

It wouldn't go well for me if any of my friends saw me. Running around the lake with Gert in her dorky white sneakers, baggy pants, and long, plaid scarf flapping in the breeze—that would be just too weird. I was counting on the fact that my friends would still be in bed where I should have been right now.

My house was right across the street from City Park Lake. A wide path circled around the lake, and it was usually crowded with dogs and their owners, kids on bikes, and couples strolling along hand-in-hand. Because this was Gert's first-ever run, I said I'd take charge of Tucker. Without a word, she handed over his braided blue leash with a plastic poop collection bag dangling from it.

We started slowly, walking side-by-side. We had the place to our-
selves. Wrinkly lines made little ditches across Gert's face. A roll
of fat round her middle jiggled as she moved. Thank goodness,
I thought, with any luck, none of my friends would ever know
about this goofy run.

Some of my classmates had grannies who walked their dogs or
played golf, but I didn't know any grannies who ran. I wondered
if it was okay for Gert to be doing this. What if she tripped and
fell and broke a hip or something?

After walking for a few minutes, I began to move a little faster,
curious to see what Gert could do. Tucker's tail wagged like
crazy. Gert stayed with me for maybe three minutes before she
slowed to a walk. That was fine with me. Speed wasn't my thing.
I was used to bringing up the rear at every cross-country workout.

My parents never came to watch my cross-country meets, even
though they were the fitness freaks who insisted that I go out for
a sport every season. I didn't think this was fair, because they
talked about fitness way more than they worked out themselves.
One time I went to the gym with my dad, and he spent most of
our time there drinking coffee and talking with his friend.

Any sport would do, they told me, but I had to do *something*. I
chose cross-country running because it seemed less terrible than
wrestling, basketball, or soccer. In those sports you had to wear

funny uniforms and tangle with lots of sweaty bodies.

Wii bowling was my secret passion. The problem was that I couldn't convince Mom and Dad that it was a real sport. So I was stuck with cross-country until I could find a way out. I was working on it.

Now that we were walking, Gert could talk, something she was very good at. Tucker and I listened. "How far is it around this lake? How long do you think it will take us? Are you getting tired?"

Before I could answer, she went on with more questions. "What does it take to get ready to run more than twenty-six miles? How can I find out?"

"It's a little over a mile around the lake, Gert, far enough for your first run. We're taking it easy, running a little, and walking a little so you don't end up gasping for breath.

To be honest, I didn't know anything about running long distances like marathons, so I couldn't offer much advice. We didn't train for marathons in cross-country. The longest we'd ever run in practice was three miles.

Gert talked on. "I'm still wondering about those runners we saw yesterday, Henry. Why do you suppose they looked so happy?"

"I bet they weren't so jolly after they'd run twenty miles." I nodded my head and frowned, letting her know that I had an idea about how it might feel to be on your feet for twenty miles and still have six to go. "I can't imagine running that far." Tucker was dragging me ahead, confident that he could outrun the squirrel he was chasing.

"No, Henry. I can't imagine it either. That's why I keep wondering about it. I want to figure out how it's done. There were so many people, and they looked so ordinary — not like buffed-up athletes. I'm thinking that it can't be as impossible as it seems."

Jogging some, then walking to allow Gert to catch her breath, we made it around the lake in less than twenty minutes. By then I was thinking breakfast. "Let's go home, Gert." If I couldn't find any Pop-Tarts in the cupboard, my plan was to eat the hot dogs I knew were stashed away in the back corner of the fridge.

When we got to my house, I poured Gert a cup of coffee, and she sat sipping it, her hands tight around her cup, while I filled up on frosted strawberry Pop Tarts and cold, but pretty good tasting hot dogs.

Gert got excited about weird projects, like learning to backpack in the wilderness, climb mountains, and play the guitar. She had lots of jobs in her life. When she was younger, she worked in a camp for refugee kids, played in a rock and roll band, and organized activities on ocean cruises. It was hard to tell what she might do next. We had only gone for one short walk-run, but I had a funny feeling that it might be the beginning of another crazy Gert project.

13

And it was looking like I was going to be the one to get sucked into joining her.

Chapter 2

Monday, when I got home from cross-country practice, Gert was at my front door. "C'mon, Henry. Let's go 'round the lake."

"I'm tired, Gert, and I have homework to do, but okay. I'll go for a short run with you." It was a safe bet none of my team would be out now, so soon after practice. I dumped my laptop on the kitchen table and grabbed a handful of peanut butter cookies, thinking I'd been right on about being a part of Gert's newest project.

This time she jogged a little more and walked a little less. It surprised me that she already seemed more relaxed and comfortable with what she was doing. Tucker chased a couple of ducks, and Gert laughed when the ducks launched themselves into the safety of the lake, leaving Tucker in the dust. When I got home, it was getting dark. There was a little time left for me to fight with some math problems before dinner.

I didn't see Gert again until Friday afternoon. I was jogging around the lake with my cross-country team. The front-runners rounded a curve and I followed several yards behind them. Then I saw her.

15

She lay stretched out on her back near the lakeshore, Tucker and her sneakers and socks alongside her in the dirt. She was soaking her feet in the mucky water. "I made it, Henry," she called when she saw me approaching. "I ran all the way around the lake."

I can't tell you how grateful I was that the rest of the team had disappeared by the time I came upon Gert. No doubt they had seen her, probably laughed at the sight of her, but there was no way for them to know that she and I had any connection.

Beautiful, I thought. *I wouldn't have to explain to anyone why this lady was talking to me.* I knew it seemed silly, and kind of mean, because I loved my granny, but I was panicked at the thought of my teammates finding out that we were related, and that I, who was so slow and knew so little about running, had become the closest thing she had to a coach.

"Whew, Henry. I worked up a sweat, even on this chilly day. And boy, do my feet hurt."

"Hey, Hank, What's up?" Toby, the heaviest of my cross-country teammates and a bit of a bully, plodded up behind me, a nasty surprise. Apparently, I wasn't dead last today.

"Hi, Toby," I said. "How goes it?" *Did he see me talking to Gert?* With a wave and a quick glance at Gert, I took off with Toby. I felt bad about leaving Gert without a word, but it was the only way I could make an escape without Toby figuring out that I knew her. I'd be in for some serious teasing if he spread the word to the team about Gert and me. I made sure to run fast enough so

16

that Toby couldn't talk and still keep up with me. In the silence broken only by our heavy breathing, we ran back to school together. I took off for home right after we arrived.

Why would it matter if the guys on the team knew I was running with Gert? Maybe it wouldn't, but I didn't want to take any chances. I took a little comfort in knowing that there was no way Toby could know that Gert was my grandmother.

On my way home, I stopped by Gert's house to check on her. "Sorry for leaving you at the lake," I called as I walked in the door. "I had to get back to school."

"It's okay, Henry. I wasn't looking my best at that moment. I wonder what your friend thought when he saw me with my feet in the lake."
"He didn't think anything at all, Gert." She didn't seem upset at my quick departure with Toby, so I decided not to say any more about it. "How are your feet?" I smiled at the fuzzy bear slippers she was wearing. "I think you need a good pair of shoes to run in. Why don't you and I take a trip to the running store this weekend?"

We headed across town to Runners Roost. A nice man had Gert try on several pairs of running shoes and walk around the store in them. He watched her stride, then nodded his head. He didn't crack a smile. I stared down at the floor.
"I'll take those pink and yellow ones." Gert's voice was even

louder when she was excited.

"You'll do better with this gray-and-white pair. They'll support your arches and they have plenty of room for your bunions." The shoe man looked serious, as if he really cared about how Gert's new shoes were going to work for her.

"What are bunions?" I asked. I'd never heard the word before. Gert showed me a boney lump sticking out from the side of both her big toes. *Ugh*, I thought. *I hope running doesn't give me those*. And then I had an idea. Maybe I could convince Mom and Dad to let me quit running so that I wouldn't risk getting any of those gross-looking bumps on my feet.

Gert rubbed her fingers over her biggest bunion. "For years I wore the fanciest, highest-heeled shoes I could find, Henry. Now I'm paying for it with these bunions." And there went my plan to get out of cross-country because of the possibility of bunions. I knew for sure that there were no high heels in my future.

"Break in your new shoes slowly," the man warned. "Don't add more than four miles a week to your training. You don't want to get injured."

On our way home, Gert treated me to a pepperoni pizza, my favorite. "Want some?" I offered.

"Sure." She ate one piece. Before she dropped me off at my house, I'd chowed down the rest. I was, after all, a growing boy. Gert didn't look like the granny I knew the next time we met to run. In new shoes, a bright-green tech shirt, and sleek, black running tights, she looked like, well, a granny on the run. She topped off her outfit with a gray-green floppy hat with a fake white rose on the side that she found at the Goodwill store. "To keep the sun off my wrinkles," she explained. In a weird way, this lady, who could so easily make me cringe with her goofiness and her never caring about what anyone thought, made me feel warm inside—even a little proud.

When Gert asked me if I'd ever wondered what it would be like to run for twenty-six-point-two miles, I said, "No, Gert. Never. For me, that's waaay too far to even think about."

"Yes. It is a long way. But I keep thinking about all the people who do it."

Chapter 3

Tucker raced ahead, excited to be off leash, when we headed to the foothills for our weekend run. Gert had been training every other day. She never talked about running a marathon, but I knew from her questions that she was thinking about it. I wasn't. I was willing to run with her so she wouldn't have to train alone, but three-mile cross-country runs were more than enough for me.

Sometimes Gert ran around the lake; other times she ran to the library, the bank, or the post office. "I love doing errands on my feet," she told me. "I've been reading about a man who ran a mile in less than five minutes when he was fifty years old. And he finished the Boston Marathon fourteen times. Imagine that, Henry."

In the distance, the Rocky Mountains shone clear and brilliant on this early fall day. Gert slowed near the top of the hill. "More air! My lungs need more air."

"I think you need more oxygen, Gert. Maybe you should take it easy. You forget that you are sixty-seven years old. Let's soak up this awesome view for a minute."

21

"I'll be okay. Just gotta catch my breath." Gert was off again before I was quite ready to go. This workout was beginning to feel like a forced march. But when we came to the downhill part, I felt like I was flying. The breeze blew through my hair. Gert threw her floppy hat to the sky, and we watched as it floated ahead of us.

"This is fun. Can you grab my hat before it gets away, Henry?"

The next weekend, when it was time for our training run, the wind sent sheets of rain sideways that made a scary splatting noise against my bedroom window. *Oh, good, a day off*, I thought. Boy was I wrong.

"Gotta go, Henry," Gert called from downstairs. She didn't ask if I wanted to run in the rain. "Track workout today," was all she said. I got my grumpy self up and out the door to slosh around the track at the high school. After forty minutes we were soaked and freezing and looked like people made from mud.

"Enough," Gert said. "Good job." We headed home.

Tucker shook himself dry — not clean, but dry. I dumped my muddy clothes on the pile by my bed and crawled back into it. "That was the longest and best hot shower of my life," Gert told me afterward.

Late that night, my phone rang. My parents had gone to bed, and I was alone in the family room sharpening up my Wii bowling skills. Gert's voice was shaky. "I'm scared, Henry. The big muscle in my calf hurts so much I can't sleep." I told her what I'd heard my coach tell runners when they had a pulled muscle.

"Take a bag of peas from the freezer and hold it on your calf for five minutes. Take a break and do it again—two or three times. Ice it again in the morning and then every few hours for a couple of days. And, Gert, no running for a while."

"What? No running? Really? I'm not going to like *that*. Tucker's not going to like it either." Uh oh. There was no doubt that Gert was seriously hooked. Who knew where this journey she had set out upon was going to take her?

Gert did not run. Instead, she walked slowly around the lake with Tucker every day. Every night she called me. After ten days, she said, "I've been icing faithfully, Henry. Do you think I can run yet? Tucker's been bugging me." I told her to give it a try.

Two days later, I saw her jogging along with Tucker, a big smile on her face. "Henry, I have news for you. I've joined a running club where I can run with lots of people. One of them gave me a whole packet of information about running a marathon. I'm learning about hard days and easy days, long runs and short runs, rest days and cross training, and what to eat. Anyone who follows this printed schedule," she said, pulling a chart out of her pocket and waving it at me, "will be able to finish a marathon. And that includes me. I'll need three months to train."

Good, I thought. The more time she took to get ready to do this crazy project of hers, the more likely she would be able to finish without falling apart. I promised to keep on running with her whenever I could. She would need to put in many more miles than I'd have time to run with her. For a moment or two, I considered asking her to work out with my cross-country team, but I quickly thought better of that idea.

Chapter 4

After a few more weeks of training, most of the workouts with her new running club friends, Gert announced that she was ready to try running in a race. "If I'm going to run in a long race with thousands of people, I need to see what it feels like to start off in a crowd and keep going until I reach a goal. Don't you think that's a good idea?"

"I guess. Some of the guys from my cross-country team are running in the Heart and Sole 5k—that's three point one miles. Maybe you should sign up for it." I cringed when I imagined Granny Gert lined up at the start with members of my team.

"Come on, Henry. Run the race with me. I'll treat you to the entry fee."

"I don't know, Gert. I've never done a road race. And I don't want to do my first one tagging along with my granny," I added under my breath.

At least Gert was looking more like an athlete these days. She wore real running shoes and tights, and now she had a fancy watch. It told her how fast she was going, how far she'd run, and even her heart rate. She loved pushing the little buttons. And she had started keeping track of her workouts on her iPad.

What could I say? It would be strange racing with Gert along with a bunch of my cross-country teammates. But she wanted to do the race so badly, and when I weighed her wishes against the chance that she might embarrass me by bumping into someone, falling down, or elbowing her way through a crowd of runners, my decision was easy. I decided to run with her.

On the day of the race, I helped Gert attach her bib number to the front of her shirt with safety pins. "Be careful, Henry, I don't want holes in my tech shirt." I showed her how to twist the little timing chip onto the lace of her shoe and set her watch to zero, ready to push a button at the start so she could see her pace per mile and know her finishing time.

"When you cross the mats at the start and finish lines, the chip will record your time. You'll be able to know your official time moments after you finish. Then you can check to see if the time on your watch matches up." I knew this much from running in cross-country meets.

"Fine. But I don't really care about how fast I go. All I want to do is finish this thing."

The race wasn't huge, perhaps a couple hundred people. Some lined up with their dogs on leashes, others got ready to push a little kid in a running stroller. A group of five guys from the cross-country team huddled together near the starting line, counting on leading the rest of the runners down the road. Gert and I lined up nearer the back of the pack.

Crack went the starting gun, and we were off in a crowd of joggers, dogs, and strollers, trying to keep from crashing into each other. Gert and I stuck together, close to the side of the road, where there was more breathing room.

"Go ahead," she told me when we stopped for a drink of water at the first aid station. "I'm fine. I'll see you at the finish."

Not sure if it was the right thing to do, I went ahead, dodging bodies left and right, trying to find a comfortable pace and avoid a collision.

"Hank, looks like you left your old lady friend behind, you speedster," Toby called from the sidelines. His friends giggled. I waved and smiled and kept on running.

When I looked at my watch as I crossed the finish line, I was surprised. I had clocked a time faster than any I'd ever done in training. And I wasn't totally breathless. How could that be?

I didn't have to wait long for Gert to show up, arms pumping, sweat dripping, and a gigantic smile on her face. She caught my eye and came over to where I was standing.

"Yahoo Henry. What a blast! All I thought about during the whole race was putting one foot in front of the other and not stopping. I just kept going until I stomped on that spongy mat at

27

the finish line. And look, there are still plenty of people coming in behind me. I wasn't even close to last."

That oh-so-good feeling after finishing an especially good run that I was beginning to experience now and then, washed over me. I was happy about my fast time, but I was even happier that Gert had done so well.

Chapter 5

I was a little bummed but not really surprised when Gert grinned and said, "Of course we're going." It was a Saturday morning, and we'd planned to run, but the wind was snapping tree branches and sending trash cans bouncing noisily down the street. At least there was no rain. It seemed like a perfect Wii bowling opportunity to me. But I agreed to go, because something inside me could not let Gert down. She was so determined to stay on her marathon training schedule.

"Tell me, Gert. Why is it so important for you to run a marathon?"

"Because it's there," she said. "And because I want to see if it is possible. If I get stronger and lose my flabby body while I'm training, that's a bonus. And one more reason: I'm having so much fun!"

We stumbled along for a couple of miles, bucking the wind with our heads down, until a gust tried its best to flip us onto our butts. "Henry . . . I quit."

Finally, I thought, *she's come to her senses*. "Okay, Gert, but there's only one way home and that's on our feet." When we turned around, the wind was a little kinder to us.

I ran with Gert whenever I could. After a while I began to notice that I wasn't the last one to finish during cross-country workouts anymore.

One day, Coach timed me and looked up, puzzled. Then out of his mouth came his favorite expression for describing an awesome accomplishment. "Rip city, Hank. You're after it. Keep up the good work."

I wasn't anywhere close to falling in love with running, but it was getting easier for me. More and more I appreciated the sense of well-being I felt after a good run. I didn't always want to do a workout, but I was never sorry after I did one. Finding a way to quit the cross-country team didn't seem so important anymore. I decided to hang in until the end of the season. I would somehow get through the district meet, and then the season would be over for me.

One day, while Gert and I were jogging down a hill near the end of a long run on a winding path through deep woods, she tripped on a tree root. She fell to the ground with a sickening thud and landed face down in the dirt. I turned around just in time to see a mountain biker barreling around the curve above us, full speed ahead. He slammed on his brakes and skidded forward, flying into the air in a tangle of spinning wheels, arms, and legs, landing squarely on top of Gert.

The biker looked up at me. "Help," he groaned, grabbing his knee and trying to pull a foot out of his clip-in pedal. I ran over. No sound from Gert. She did not move.

"Okay," I yelled, "but first, get off my granny." I grabbed the biker under his arms and lifted him enough so that I could drag him and his bike away from Gert.

"I think maybe I broke something," he mumbled. Blood streamed from his calf. One leg of his biking pants was torn away. A big scraped area of skin, filled with dirt and pebbles, oozed blood.

I moved him to a grassy spot and left him to untangle himself. Gert lay motionless on her stomach, eyes closed, her face turned to the side, a scary shade of gray, all scratched up and bleeding. The area around a bloody gash on her upper arm and elbow was already turning purple. It was her stillness that scared me most.

I grabbed the water bottle from its cage on the bike and squeezed it into Gert's face. She moved her head a little and opened her eyes. "Ummm . . . what happened?" I could barely understand her. "Where am I? Whatever happened?" Tucker whined and licked her face.

"You were just in the wrong place at the wrong time, Gert. You're going to be okay. I promise. Keep still for me, okay?"

Relief flooded through me. Thank God. At least she was alive. I didn't usually carry my cell phone when I ran, but this day I'd slipped it into my pocket because we were going on a longer-than-usual run. *Someone up there likes me*, I told myself as I dialed home. Thankfully, Mom answered.

"Gert had an accident on the trail," I told her.

"Shall I call 911?" she asked.

"I don't know, Mom. Please just come, and fast." I gave her directions to where we were on the trail.

"I'm on my way," she said.

The mountain biker had managed to get himself together some. He had found a greasy rag to wrap around his bleeding calf. "So sorry," he said. "Never saw the lady until it was too late. I hope she's going to be all right. If I could do something to help, I would, but with this painful leg, I'm no good to anyone."

"My mom's on the way. Do you think you can get yourself down the hill?"

"I'll make it. I don't live far from here." The biker lifted his battered machine into an upright position and began limping down the trail. "I hope she's okay," he called again as he disappeared.

"Henry? Gert?" my mother called out.

"Over here," I shouted. "Just around the curve."

Mom hurried up the trail, carrying a bulging first aid kit. "Oh,

Gert, what kind of crazy thing have you done now?"

"Don't worry, sweetie," Gert said, her voice soft and small for once. "Just a few scratches and a headache." Mom knelt down beside her and took her pulse. She'd always been good at doctor stuff. She checked Gert over, inch-by-inch, gently moving her arms and legs and inspecting her head, neck, and shoulders.

"Miracle," Mom said. "Nothing's broken, Gert, but you're not going to be running for quite a while. You've got a huge gash and bruise on your arm, you're going to have a black eye, there's a big bump on the back of your head, and a scrape on your fore-head. I can't tell until we get your running pants off what's going on with your leg."   Then she cleaned the wound on Gert's arm and wrapped it tightly to stop the flow of blood.

It wasn't pretty, the way Mom and I half-carried, half-dragged Gert to the car as carefully as we could. Mom grabbed a blanket to cover her and I folded up my coat to make a pillow for her head. I climbed in beside her and rested her head on my knee to steady her for the trip home. Tucker settled in quietly at my feet.

Before we got to my house, Gert mumbled, "I bruise easy. It looks a lot worse than it is. Give me a few days and I'll be as good as new."

A few hours later, we took Gert back to her house, all bandaged up and looking like a wounded warrior. I didn't want to think about how stiff and achy she was going to be the next morning. We helped her onto the living room couch, not even attempting to get her upstairs and into her own bed.

"Call me in the morning before you try to get up," Mom said. "I mean it, Gert."

"Do you think she'll be able to run the marathon?" I asked Mom as we headed home.

"We'll see how fast she heals." Mom looked doubtful. "I know your granny is tough, but cuts and bruises take longer to heal when you're older. We'll just have to wait and see."

Chapter 6

W hen I went over to Gert's the next day, I found her under a quilt on the couch. She hardly moved when I came in, but she managed a weak smile.

"Gert, I got to thinking that maybe you tripped near the end of the run because you needed food and water. Coach always tells us to drink before we're thirsty and eat before we're hungry." I felt a little funny, offering her this advice.

"Maybe so. I'll see what I can do," she answered in a quiet voice. She was too quiet, and I wondered if she had given up her plan. Neither of us mentioned the marathon.

A week later, on my way home from cross-country practice, I ran into Gert on the path by the lake. A purple, green, and yellow bruise covered most of one leg and an arm. Her elbow was still bandaged. The scrape on her forehead had begun to heal, but was still fiery red, and her black eye had faded only a little. She wore a belt around her waist with little pockets to hold food and drink.

She took slow, small steps. Every one looked painful. But she didn't have any trouble talking about the gel packets, power bars, chock blocks, and energy drinks she'd discovered. "These blocks taste great, Henry. They're like supersized gumdrops."

"Hmmm. I'll try a red one. Thanks. I could use a quick shot of energy."

By October, orange, yellow and gold leaves covered the path around the lake. Slowly, oh so slowly, Gert and I began to run together again. "Start slow and taper off," I told Gert.

She laughed. "What in the world does that mean?"

"It means take it easy, Gert. Just take it easy." She gave me one of her special looks, as if to say, *Don't tell me what to do.*

Every day Gert went a little farther and a little faster. Neither of us said anything about the marathon, but it wasn't long before I knew that Gert had decided to go ahead with it. When I saw her that day limping along with her new belt full of food and drinks, I figured she wasn't going to let a major wipeout and a face-off with a mountain bike keep her from her goal.

In time we worked up to twelve and then fifteen-mile runs. I'd never dreamed, never wanted, to go that far. The district cross-country meet, where five schools competed for a chance to go to state, was coming right up, and I began to wonder whether all the extra miles I'd been putting in would make a difference. Our runs were never fast, but we were consistent, and the miles were piling up.

We ran a twenty-miler because Gert's schedule said she had to.
No one said I had to. In fact, I was almost certain Coach would
not have recommended it, but I couldn't imagine Gert going
alone. We took plenty of food and water, and at mile ten we
walked a little.
"We're halfway there, Henry. How goes it with you?"

"I'm done in. How about you?"

"I can't imagine doing another ten, but let's go."

We struggled through the last few miles, legs aching, feet sore,
but we didn't let each other quit.

Afterward, we celebrated with enormous chocolate milkshakes.
"The more you run, the more you can eat and not get fat, isn't
that right, Gert?" I toasted her, holding my milkshake high. She
pulled up her shirt, right there at McDonald's, and tried to grab
the skin around her middle. She had a hard time grabbing hold of
much.

"See, this flab is disappearing right before my eyes."

I tried not to laugh. "Gert, keep your shirt on. People will think
you're loony."

Chapter 7

"I can hardly wait until your district cross-country meet, Henry. I want to see what the new Henry body can do."

There was a time when I would have hoped Gert would not show up at my district meet. I would have worried about her loud voice and what she might say to the coach or the kids. But no longer. She was my running buddy, and I was proud to have her come. As far as I was concerned, she could say or do whatever she liked, and as loud as she liked, and it wouldn't bother me one bit.

Over the past weeks, Gert had probably learned a few things about running from me, but I had learned so much from her that I found myself developing a whole new attitude, and not just about running. She was so strong and determined, so confident about what she could do, and so unafraid to ask for what she needed. She treated everyone the same way, and she didn't much care what anyone thought about her. Things that once seemed so important to me, like who I hung out with and what they thought about me, now seemed silly.

Toby spotted Gert at the start of the district meet. "Hey, Hank, your runner-granny is here." Gert was hard to miss in her new shocking-pink tech shirt, a souvenir of the 5-k race she'd run. And, of course, she wore her floppy hat with the white rose on the side.

By this time, Gert and I had been training together for so long that everyone knew she was my granny, and I liked that they did.

"You've got your own cheering section, Hank. How lucky for you."

"Yeah, I know, Toby. Maybe she'll bring us both some luck."

A strange thing happened as I stood waiting at the start. All of a sudden, I had this overwhelming feeling, this compulsion, to go for it—to do my very best. That was a feeling I'd never had before.

Buck, the fastest guy on our team, would be going on to high school next year. This was his last middle school meet unless we qualified for state. He kept twitching, jumping up and down, running around in little circles, and chattering about the course made slick by the damp grass.

Not me. I didn't say a word, and I didn't move a muscle. My palms were sweaty, and my heart was thump, thump, thumping. I felt as if I was about to bungee jump into a canyon, a feeling totally new to me. I was used to showing up at meets because I had to. But today I wanted to be there—I *needed* to be there—and I wanted to say to those lined up with me, "Watch out. Here I come!"

I thought about Gert and the hours she'd spent running over the last months, just to find out if she could complete a marathon. And I thought about Coach's advice, even though I didn't pay much attention to him at times. "Don't hold back at the start. In a three-mile race, there's no time for catch-up and no room for error. Attack the first hill with all you've got."

Hill attack. Okay.

"Watch your tangents. There are lots of turns on the course. Find the shortest distance from one point to another, and make sure you are in position to take advantage of it."

Cut corners. Okay.

At the sound of the starting gun, I took off with Coach's words echoing in my head. Tackling the first hill, I realized that an all-out effort for three miles wasn't going to happen. I needed to find my fastest comfortable pace and stay with it. The tight pack of runners spread out. With some maneuvering room, I felt more confident. I didn't waste time looking back. Instead, I concentrated on the job I had to do.

When I did look up, I saw a sign that said a half-mile to go. There were three runners ahead of me. *Strange*, I thought. *Where is everybody? Did I miss a turn?*

As the finish line came close, I saw Gert and Coach cheering, and

41

I dug deep in search of a final burst of speed. Ahead of me, Buck crossed the line and bent over, gasping. Within seconds I was doing the same.

"Second place, Henry. You took second for our team and fourth overall. And you did a personal best by almost four minutes. Bravo!"

I heard Coach's words as if they came from somewhere deep in a hollow tunnel. *Were they real? Were they meant for me? Second on our team? Fourth overall? Really?*

"Fantastic job." Coach put his arm around me. "I don't think you know how important this is, Henry. It's going to give us the points we need to qualify for state."

"Thanks, Coach," were the only words I could come up with. I turned to Gert, who was jabbering to Tucker, something about her hero.

"Thanks for the training runs, Gert. And thanks for being here." She wrapped her arms around me in a monster hug. I didn't care who saw her hugging me, but I was glad she didn't do something crazy like trying to pick me up and whirl me around.

Chapter 8

The night before Gert's marathon, she asked me to sleep over at her house. Even though she'd set three alarms, she was afraid she wouldn't wake up in time to get to the race which started at 6:30 a.m. This made no sense to me. She always got up early, and she never needed an alarm to wake her up.

That granny of mine swore she did not sleep that night, even for a minute. I heard snoring once, but maybe I dreamed it. At 4:30 a.m., I heard her get up, and I knew she was following the routine we'd planned: stretch, drink water, and eat a banana and half a bagel with peanut butter. She didn't want me to come to the start with her. "Way too early," she'd said. "It would be silly."

"Are you sure?"

"Absolutely. But please meet me at the finish with Tucker. You may need to pick up whatever's left of me."

I got up before the sun rose on a chilly November morning, a little cold for spectating but perfect for running. Tucker was ready to go. I knew that Gert must have been shivering with goose bumps at the start caused by the cold, and by nervousness.

43

I checked my watch as Tucker and I set out for the race course.

In my head, I was right there with Gert. All those thousands of runners must have been delighted to hear the gun go off and be moving on down the long road, warming up at last. I'd never done a marathon, but I knew what it was like to run for twenty miles, and I couldn't imagine running twenty-six-plus without some worries about how it was going to turn out in the end.

Gert and I had lots of time to talk during our long runs. In the last couple of weeks, she had shared her thoughts and her fears. "It's the unknown that makes it so enticing," she said. "If you've never done it before, how can you know how your body will behave when it must go that far? I'm planning to take it one mile at a time. That's all I can do."

I rode my bike to mile eight where I spotted Gert as she reached into her little belt and popped a chock block into her mouth. She didn't see me. Long-distance racing wasn't much of a spectator sport, but Tucker and I found a few good spots on the loop course where we could watch for her and cheer her on.

Every two miles or so, runners paused at aid stations to drink. Some used the Porta Potties; others found their way to a medical tent offering help for blisters. The course wound around and looped back on itself so that I arrived at mile twenty-one in time to see a lot of runners go by. But I didn't see Gert.

When the time seemed about right, I biked toward the finish line and stationed myself in the crowd of spectators, close to a barrier I knew Gert would pass before she finished. Tucker and I stood together, watching runners stream by. When they crossed the finish line, timing chips were clipped from their shoes, finishing medals were hung around their necks, and then they went in search of food, drink, friends, and rest.

Time passed. I told myself not to worry. Runners were still pouring across the finish line. The clock was creeping up on five-and-a-half hours. Such a longtime to be pounding the pavement, I thought.

Tucker and I paced up and down the last yards of the course, watching and waiting, not sure what to think.

And then she came into view, plodding along, head up, looking around as if she were searching for us. "Over here, Gert!" I called. "You're nearly finished!" When she saw us, she managed a big smile and a wave, floppy hat in her hand.

"Tucker, Gert made it!" That dog knew exactly what was going on. Gert had her chip removed, a medal hung around her neck, then blended into the mob of people who limped around, cheered, and hugged each other. They helped themselves to water, bagels, cookies, and orange slices. Some cried. A few lay on the ground, not yet ready to speak or move.

It must have been a great happiness swelling up inside her that made Gert swing into a little dance, her shiny medal swaying gently around her neck. That was the moment when I grabbed my tired, sweaty granny and whirled her around in a victory hug for all the world to see. She was small, but solid, and she weighed more than I'd thought. I almost toppled over. I put her down. Tucker wiggled his whole body and licked her salty legs.

I looked Gert over. The fat around her middle was gone, and the wrinkles on her face hardly showed, hidden by her tan and her smile. The bunions on her feet had not kept her from her goal.

Was there anyone in the world with a granny as cool as mine?

"I wonder . . ." she said, looking me in the eye. And then she caught herself. "Maybe I'd better be careful what I wonder about next."

"Yes," I agreed. "You should watch your wondering."

But I found myself doing a little wondering of my own. Very soon, I thought to myself, I'm going to check on how old you need to be to enter the Boston Marathon.

I put my arm around Gert's shoulder, picked up my bike, and we headed through the crowd toward home. The sun peaked high in the sky, the mountains gleamed in the distance, and Tucker ran ahead of us.

Gert and I walked, side-by-side.

Appendix

Keep Track of Your Running

Recording the miles you run, your pace, and how you felt can help you track your progress and adjust your training as you become more proficient. Keep it simple so that you'll continue your record keeping.

It can be as simple as noting your mileage on a calendar or you can get more detailed by creating a log that looks like the one below on lined paper in a spiral notebook. Repeat the chart for each week of training.

Week	Date	Day	Miles	Time	Pace	Route	Notes
1		Sun					
		Mon					
		Tue					
		Wed					
		Thur					
		Fri					
		Sat					

Pacing Chart

Working toward keeping an even pace all the way through a race is a good goal. Figuring out your pace per mile will help you understand what pace you should be setting for yourself, and in the end will help to improve your time.

The far left column gives time per mile. Read horizontally across the chart to see the time you need to maintain to achieve a chosen goal.

Time/Mile	5k	5 mi	10k	15k	10 mi	½ mar
5:30	17:05	27:30	34:11	51:16	55:00	1:12:06
6:00	18:39	30:00	37:17	55:56	1:00:00	1:18:39
6:30	20:12	32:30	40:23	1:00:35	1:05:00	1:25:13
7:00	21:45	35:00	43:30	1:05:15	1:10:00	1:31:46
7:30	23:18	37:30	46:36	1:09:54	1:15:00	1:38:19
8:00	24:51	40:00	49:43	1:14:34	1:20:00	1:44:52
8:30	26:25	42:30	52:49	1:19:14	1:25:00	1:51:26
9:00	27:58	45:00	55:56	1:23:53	1:30:00	1:57:59
9:30	29:31	47:30	59:02	1:28:33	1:35:00	2:04:32
10:00	31:04	50:00	1:02:08	1:33:13	1:40:00	2:11:05
10:30	32:37	52:30	1:05:15	1:37:52	1:45:00	2:17:39
11:00	34:11	55:00	1:02:21	1:42:32	1:50:00	2:24:12
11:30	35:44	57:30	1:11:28	1:47:11	1:55:00	2:30:45
12:00	37:17	1:00:00	1:14:34	1:51:51	2:00:00	2:37:18
12:30	38:50	1:02:30	1:17:41	1:56:31	2:05:00	2:43:52
13:00	40:23	1:05:00	1:20:47	2:01:10	2:10:00	2:50:25